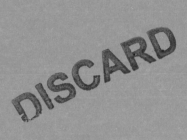

my new MOM & ME

renata galindo

schwartz & wade books · new york

When I first came to live with
my new mom, I was nervous.
This would be my home.

I'd never had my
own room before.

I was worried that I didn't look like Mom,

so I tried to fix it.

But Mom said I didn't need fixing.

She likes that we
are different.

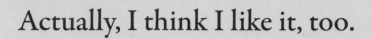

Actually, I think I like it, too.

(And who cares what anyone else thinks!)

Mom plays with me,

and she takes care of me.

She does all the things that moms do—

even the things that make me mad!

Sometimes I don't like Mom.

Sometimes I feel really sad.

But Mom promises me we'll be okay.

She says that if we just try a little harder,

tomorrow will be better.

. . . and it is!

Mom is learning how to be my mom,
and I am learning how to be Mom's kid.

We are learning how to be a family.

For Maribel and Chuy,
and for new families of all kinds

Visit us on the Web! randomhousekids.com
Educators and librarians, for a variety of teaching tools,
visit us at RHTeachersLibrarians.com
Library of Congress Cataloging-in-Publication Data
TK
The text of this book is set in Garamond Premier Pro.
The illustrations were rendered digitally.
MANUFACTURED IN CHINA
10 9 8 7 6 5 4 3 2 1
First Edition